This book belongs to:

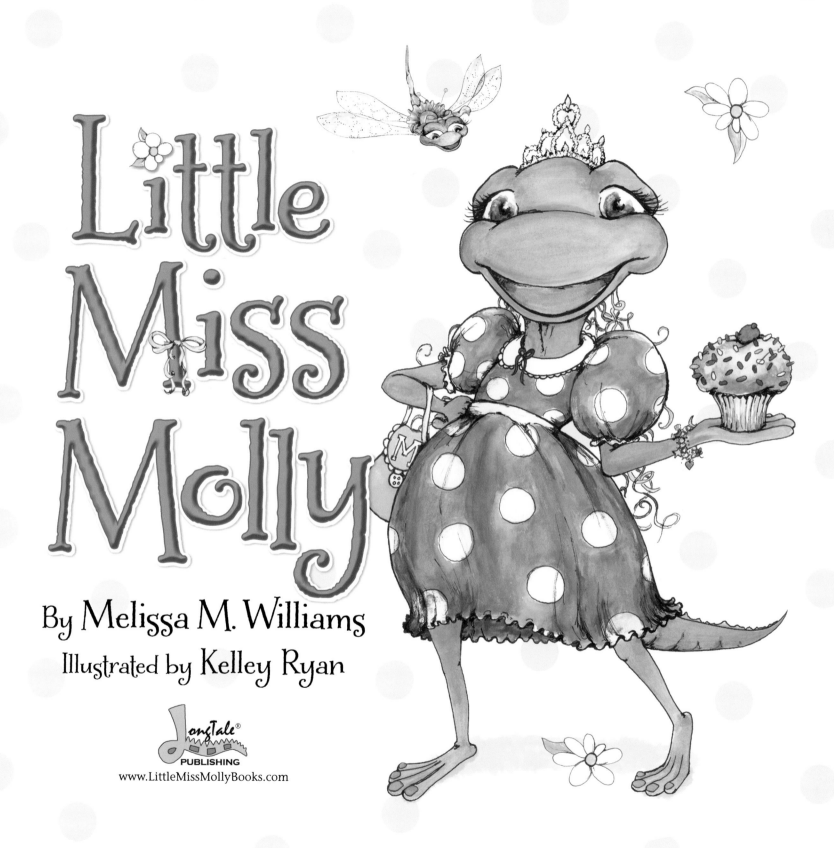

# Little Miss Molly

By Melissa M. Williams

Illustrated by Kelley Ryan

LongTale
PUBLISHING

www.LittleMissMollyBooks.com

Of all the colors in the world, Little Miss Molly loved the color pink. Bright pink, light pink, hot pink, magenta and her ultimate favorite, Princess Pink. All princesses wear Princess Pink.

Her room was pink. Her dresses were pink. Even her pet dragonfly's bow was pink. That's Tink. She's a princess, too...a fairy princess.

Pink flowers for **planting**.

Pink tutus for **dancing**.

Pink ribbons and bows for **tying**.

She even had pink
pompoms for
**cheering!**

For special occasions,
Molly wore a lovely
shade of pink
lip gloss.

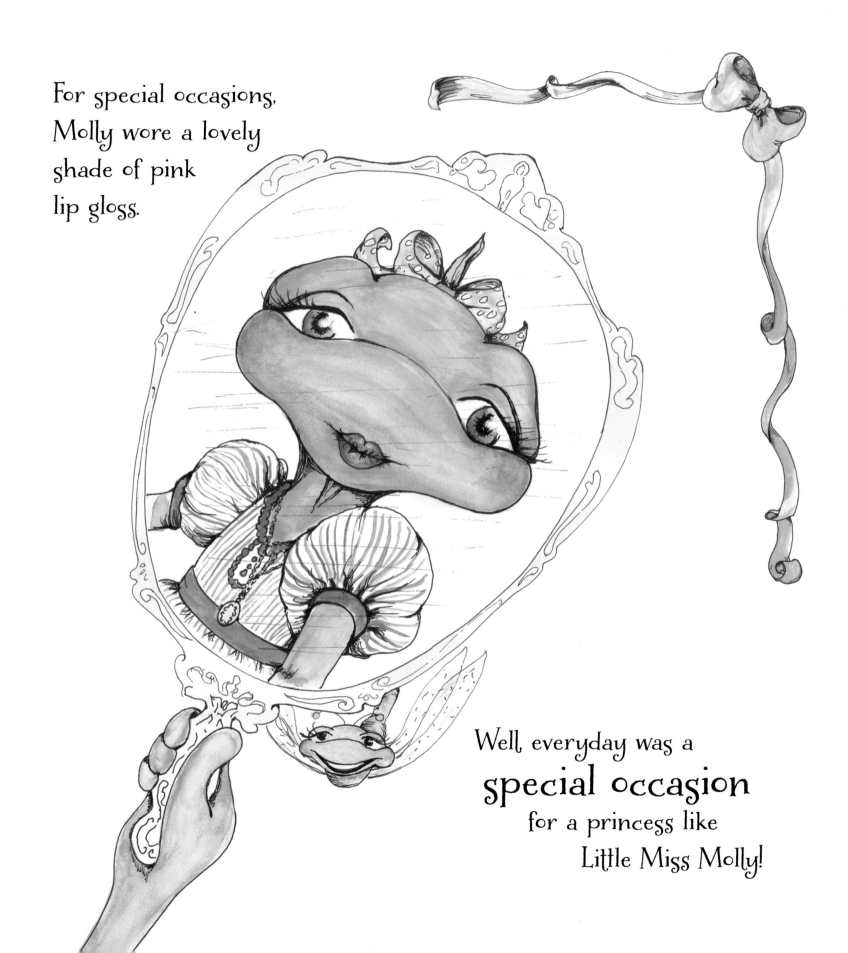

Well, everyday was a
**special occasion**
for a princess like
Little Miss Molly!

After ballet class, knowing how much Molly loved dragonflies, her mom held up a green dress with flowers and dragonflies all over. "Wouldn't you like to try another color?" she asked Molly.

"But Mother, I'm a princess. I only wear pink!" she said and leaped across her bedroom. Molly loved the attention her pink ensemble always brought and vowed never to wear another color. Tink vowed to only wear pink too.

So each and every morning, Molly arrived at school dressed in pink, pink and more pink. All of her classmates noticed her fashionable style.

"That's a pretty pink purse,"
Katie Cat said.

Molly curtsied. "Why thank you."

"Is that pink nail polish you're wearing?"
Billie Goat asked.

Molly held out her hand, "Why yes," and
batted her eyelashes. "It's called Priss 'n Pink."

"I love your pink tutu!" her best friend
Little Bit Turtle said.

Molly performed an arabesque and
leaped to her desk with a smile.

Everyday, the bunny rabbit twins, Britton and Beckett asked, "Why do you always wear pink, Molly? Why just one color?

Yuuuuck!"

Molly always told them the same thing. "Princesses only wear pink. That's why."

One night while Molly and Tink were reading a bedtime fairytale about their favorite things, princesses and fairies, her mother tried again. "Look what I found," her mother beamed. "A new blue dress for your special day!" Tomorrow was Molly's birthday.

Molly looked up from her book and bedtime snack. She still insisted, "No way! A princess must always wear the color pink. Look, it shows it right here in my book."

Her mother shook her head and collected Molly's clothes for the wash.

"Where are you taking my pink dresses and gowns?" Molly asked.

"Princesses must always wear clean clothes too," her mom answered with a smile.

On the morning of Molly's birthday, she woke up Tink and leaped to her closet to find her FAVORITE pink dress with the white polka dots. But the dress was nowhere to be found.

Tink sat on Molly's shoulder as she searched and searched.
Then she remembered her mom had taken her dirty clothes
for the wash. She ran downstairs and opened up the dryer...

"OH NO!" Molly screamed.
She pulled out her favorite dress. "Purple?"

All of her pink clothes inside the dryer had
turned purple.

Her mother arrived to see Molly holding the purple dress, tears running down her face. Mrs. Green looked inside the dryer and found a navy blue sock. "I'm sorry dear. It looks like your brother's baseball sock was washed with your pink things. It dyed everything purple."

Molly's big brother, Iggy, crept back upstairs before he got blamed.

"Purple is pretty too dear." Mrs. Green helped Molly put on her purple polka dotted dress, but Molly was not happy. Princesses wear pink.

Molly arrived at school with a beautiful birthday crown on her head. She looked just like a princess. But no one noticed the fabulous pink ribbons hanging from Molly's crown. Instead, everyone was shocked that Molly was NOT wearing pink.

Then Molly noticed that Katie was wearing a princess PINK rhinestone collar. Hot PINK dangly earrings hung from Billie's little horns. Little Bit had a pretty PINK bow on the top of her head. Even Molly's teacher, Mrs. Puff, was wearing a PINK poodle skirt.

Molly's cheeks burned bright pink. "Noooo!" Molly screamed, "You all can't wear pink!"

"Why?" Little Bit asked. "I thought you liked pink."

"I do, and it's MY favorite color!" Molly's lip quivered as she looked down at her purple dress. Then the tears came.

Mrs. Puff walked up to Molly, knelt down beside her, and asked, "What's wrong dear?"

Molly whimpered, "Everyone is wearing Princess Pink except me!"

Mrs. Puff told the little lizard, "Everyone brought something pink to surprise you for your birthday."

"But I don't want to share my favorite color!" Molly grumbled.

Mrs. Puff whispered in Molly's ear, "The prettiest princesses are the ones who share their favorite things."

Molly sat on the ground and pouted while she thought about all of her favorite princesses and how nice they were to others.

The twins walked up to Molly and handed her two pink tulips. "Happy Birthday!" they said.

"Really? For me?" Molly stood up and sniffed the tulips.

"Yes!" Britton and Beckett laughed. "We don't even like pink."

Molly wiped her tears away just as the door opened. In came her mother and Tink with pink birthday cupcakes, each adorned with Molly's favorite fruit...a green olive.

"Hooray!" the class yelled.

Molly's mom kissed her and handed her a bright pink bag. Molly untied the fancy curly-Q ribbons and pulled out a brand new princess pink dress.

"Aren't you going to go put it on?" Little Bit asked.

Molly looked around the room at all of the pink things her friends brought to school and smiled saying,

"Don't you know... Princesses also wear purple!"

Molly put down her new dress and began passing out all of the pink cupcakes to her classmates. Tink helped too.

That afternoon, Molly invited all of her friends to come over for a birthday tea party. It was a party fit for a princess. For the first time, Little Miss Molly didn't mind sharing all of her pink toys, costumes and teacups. Everyone wore pink too, except Molly. She wore purple.

~The End~

# Visit Molly's website for your very own Molly doll and goodies!

Be sure to keep a lookout for more tips on how you can become a princess too!

## www.LittleMissMollyBooks.com

## Other books by the author

include the *Iggy the Iguana* and *Turtle Town* chapter book series.

Iggy the Iguana

Turtle Town

www.IggytheIguana.com
www.TurtleTownBooks.com

## For more information

about school visits, workshops and public speaking requests:

E-mail Melissa at
melissa@longtalepublishing.com
or Online at
www.MelissaMWilliamsAuthor.com

Support Literacy through reading and writing:
www.READ3Zero.org

Conquering illiteracy together...

READ 3

...30 minutes at a time

# About the Author and Illustrator

MELISSA M. WILLIAMS spent her childhood years using her imagination, creating stories and acting out character skits with her little sister. Some of her favorite memories, besides playing make-believe, revolved around dressing up her pet iguanas and turtles. Melissa began teaching and working with children while completing her Master's Degree in professional counseling, which has influenced many of the lessons found in her stories. In addition to *Little Miss Molly*, Melissa's works include the *Iggy the Iguana* and *Turtle Town* chapter book series. Over the years, Melissa has had the chance to work with many talented student-writers and in 2009 founded the Literacy Non-Profit Foundation, READ3Zero, giving children the opportunity to become published authors. Melissa currently lives in Houston, Texas, where she regularly visits schools and speaks to students about the world of creative writing.

KELLEY RYAN's passion for art emerged at a very young age, crediting her mother for such an amazing and inherited gift. Kelley grew up in Texas and received a Bachelors of Fine Art from Texas State University with an emphasis in painting. Kelley currently lives in Manhattan, New York where she spends much of her time painting for clients and galleries. Her pop art portraits are being shown at Galerie Élysées. Kelley's unique characters and illustrations can be found inside the colorful pages of *Little Miss Molly*, in addition to the *Iggy the Iguana* and *Turtle Town* chapter book series for kids. To view the artist's work, visit the Kelley Ryan Gallery at kelleyryangallery.com.

To my little sister, Michele.
Our childhood created this character.

Little Miss Molly
Copyright © 2013 by Melissa M. Williams. All rights reserved.
ISBN 978-0-9854705-1-7
Library of Congress Control Number: 2012917783

PUBLISHING

Published by Long Tale Publishing
www.LongTalePublishing.com
6824 Long Drive Houston, Texas 77087

LongTale® is a registered trademark of LongTale Publishing.

Illustrations by Kelley Ryan, *kelleyryangallery.com*.
Design by Monica Thomas for TLC Graphics, *www.TLCGraphics.com*.

First Edition
Printed in the United States of America.